The Adventu Trunksy and Peanut

By
Megan Skokovic

Illustrated by Graziella Miligi

The Adventures of Trunksy and Peanut

Once upon a time there was a young Helmet Vanga bird named Peanut. He lived with his mom, dad, brothers and sisters up in the tall trees in the jungle.

Peanut wasn't your average baby bird. In fact, he was much less than average. Peanut was born very small and often times got made fun of because of his size or lack thereof.

One day, Peanut was flying with his parents
when they stopped at a watering hole where
many elephants were gathered around.

As they approached the cool pool of water, Peanut's mother held him close because she was afraid the elephants wouldn't see him and he would get squashed.

While Peanut and his parents were getting a sip of water, Peanut noticed a baby elephant with an exceptionally large trunk getting a drink across the pond.

As all the grownups began talking, Peanut was able to slip away. He flew over to the long trunked elephant and landed on his trunk.

"Hi my name is Peanut!" He said.
"Hi I'm Trunksy." Said the elephant shyly.
"You've got a great big trunk for your size!"
Peanut exclaimed.

"Yeah well at least I'm bigger than a dung beetle."
Trunksy snapped.
"Oh, I'm sorry, I didn't mean anything by it!"
Peanut could tell his new friend had been made
fun of in the past.

"I think your trunk is cool! You can use it as a snorkel and go all the way down to the bottom of the lake!" Peanut said.

Trunksy looked up with excitement in his eyes. "I do that all the time! It's my favorite activity!" He said proudly.

"How come you're so small?" Said the now happier elephant.

"I've always been like this." Peanut said sadly
as tears filled his eyes.

As tears began rolling down Peanut's cheeks, Trunksy grabbed a small leaf so Peanut could wipe his eyes. "I know I am very small, but it isn't all bad. There are things I can do that my brothers and sisters can't." Peanut said wiping his tears away.

"Like what?" Asked Trunksy. "Well when we are trying find dinner as a family, I am very good at fitting into small spaces to flush insects out straight to my parents." Peanut began to smile at the thought of his special trick.

"Wow! That's awesome, I bet your family really loves that." The elephant stated emphatically. "It is pretty cool, I guess." Peanut shrugged.

Just then, there was a screech from the trees above.

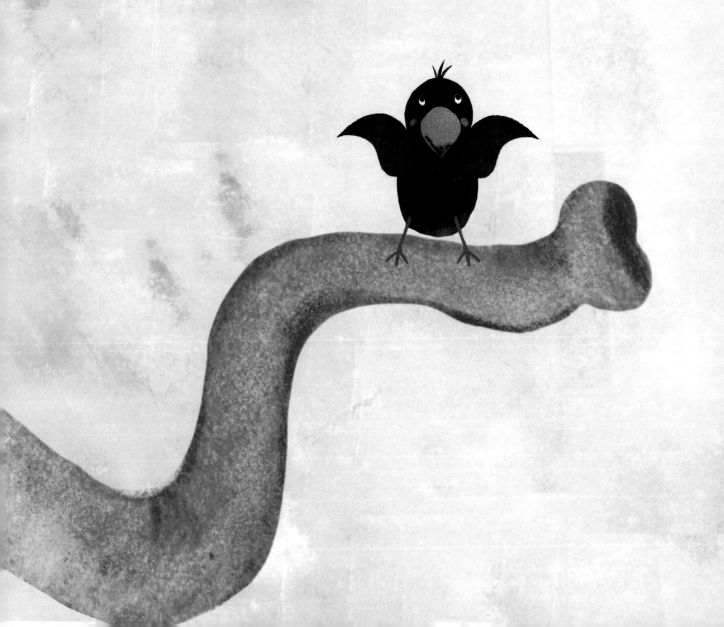

There was a baby monkey separated from his parents and he was barely hanging onto the branch.

Looking around at the panicked onlookers, Peanut and Trunksy took quick action to save the baby monkey.

"Quick! Jump in my trunk and I'll shoot you up
to the monkey! You should fit perfectly!"
Ordered the frantic elephant.
"Okay!" Peanut said as he climbed into the end
of the long trunk.

Just then, Trunksy let out a big blow of air and Peanut was shot up to the tree at great speed. He then carried a vine in his beak over to the monkey where he was able to swing back to his family.

The less than perfect pair were heroes.
All the animals and their families
cheered in excitement for the duo.

Peanut and Trunksy, an unlikely friend-
ship, looked at each other proudly as they
celebrated their unique abilities. They
were best friends from that day forward.

The End

About the Author:

Megan Skokovic is a loving wife and mother of her two amazing daughters. Megan has been working with children since she was very young and is currently an elementary physical education teacher. She has a passion for helping her students to grow and be successful in all areas of their lives. Megan is also a lover of nature and animals, especially the ocean. Her hope is that this book helps individuals celebrate who they are and take pride in their abilities.

43887339R00017